EGMONT

We bring stories to life

First published in Great Britain in 2007 by Dean,
an imprint of Egmont UK Limited
239 Kensington High Street, London W8 6SA

Thomas the Tank Engine & Friends™

CREATED BY BRITT ALLCROFT

HiT entertainment

ISBN 978 0 6035 6250 1
7 9 10 8 6
Printed in Singapore

Trouble for Thomas

The Thomas TV Series

DEAN

It was Christmas on the Island of Sodor.

The weather was very cold, but the engines didn't mind. There was plenty of work to do, with passengers and parcels to be delivered.

And the stations looked very jolly with all their decorations!

"We'll soon be wearing our snowploughs," said James.

"You'll enjoy that, won't you Thomas?" teased Henry.

"You know I won't," sighed Thomas. "Mine doesn't fit!" He wished he didn't have to wear a snowplough at all.

That night the wind blew around the sheds, and the snow fell very heavily.

Next morning, The Fat Controller came to the sheds. He told the engines that it was time to have their snowploughs fitted. Then he went up to Thomas.

"Thomas, I want you to collect something special from Callan Station. It's needed for the village feast on Toby's branch line."

Thomas was very excited about his special job.
But not about his snowplough!

"Please, Sir," peeped Thomas. "My plough is so
awkward and heavy. May I have one the right size?"

"We don't have any spare snowploughs," said The
Fat Controller. "You will just have
to make do."

The Fitters, the Driver and the Fireman all helped to put on Thomas' snowplough. It took a very long time because it kept dropping off!

"Big, horrid, silly thing," Thomas grumbled.

At last the snowplough was fitted and Thomas set off for Callan Station.

Thomas felt much happier when he arrived at Callan Station and saw his special delivery. It was a beautiful Christmas tree!

"The tree is going to have lights on it, and stand in the middle of the village," explained Edward. "Make sure you get it to Toby safely!"

"I will!" said Thomas, excitedly. He set off straight away.

When Thomas arrived at Maithwaite, Toby was very happy to see him.

"I'm glad you have your snowplough," said Toby. "I need to get the tree to the village, and I can't clear the snowdrifts by myself."

So Thomas went first and Toby followed him.

Thomas' snowplough wasn't working very well, because it was such a bad fit.

But he was determined to deliver the tree safely!

Suddenly, Thomas' snowplough hit something hard.

There was a huge rock buried under the snow on the track.

The metal creaked!

The bolts snapped!

"Bouncing buffers!" exclaimed Thomas. "My plough is broken!"

The broken plough hit a water tower next to the track, and the water tower tumbled down!

"Cinders and ashes!" exclaimed Thomas.

"We can't go any further," said Thomas' Driver. "And there's no one to help us."

"But the villagers need their tree," said Thomas. "Let me try again. I'm sure I can make it!"

It wasn't easy without a snowplough, but Thomas was determined. He pushed and he pushed and he pushed.

There were lots of big snowdrifts. Thomas pushed through each one. Toby followed on behind, wishing that he could help.

At last, Thomas and Toby pulled into the village station.

Thomas whistled happily and all the villagers cheered!

Next day, The Fat Controller came to see the engines. Thomas was very worried.

What would The Fat Controller say about his broken snowplough?

But The Fat Controller wasn't cross at all! "You were very brave to take on that snow without a plough," he said to Thomas.

"Thank you, Sir," chuffed Thomas.

"There are no spare snowploughs, so . . . you'll just have to make do without one!" added The Fat Controller.

"Oh, thank you, Sir!" grinned Thomas. It was just what he had wanted!